The Birthday Party

Helen Oxenbury

WALKER BOOKS
AND SUBSIDIARIES
LONDON · BOSTON · SYDNEY

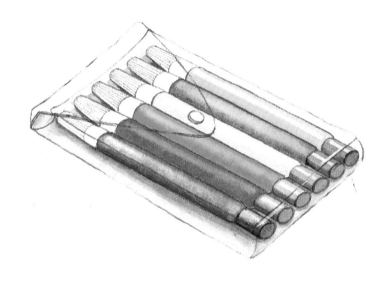

I chose John's birthday
present on my own.

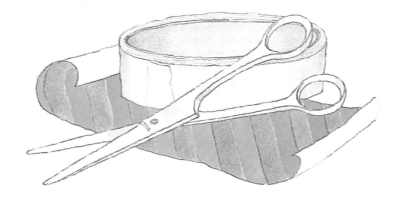

'Can't I try them out, Mum?'
'No,' Mum said, 'we bought
   them for John.'

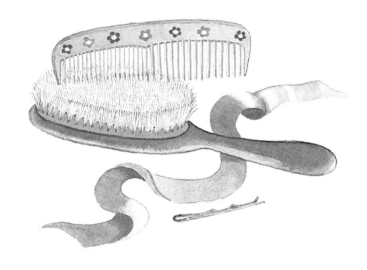

'Let's have your blue
ribbon as well,' Mum said.

'Is that my present?'
John said when we arrived.

'Happy birthday, John,'
Mum said.
She made me give him
the present.

'Here's my cake,' John shouted.
He just left my present
on the floor.

After tea we had games and
balloons and running about
and jumping and bumping.

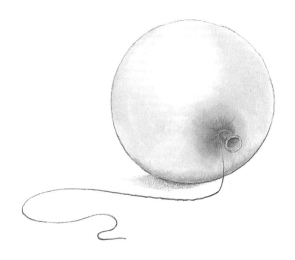

My dad collected me.
'Give her the balloon,'
John's mum said.
'Do you really want it?'
John said.
'Yes please,' I said. 'I do.'